D0244017

This book belongs to

sparkle town fairies

ROSIE
the
RUBY Fairy
and the Christmas Mail Mix-Up

Sarah Creese * Lara Ede

make
believe
ideas

In **Sparkle Town**, on Ruby Hill,
towering, tall and proud,
there stood a bustling **Post Office**
with spires that reached the clouds.

In **charge** of sorting all the post,
each parcel, card and letter,

SORTING ROOM

was **Rosie** the **Ruby Fairy** –
no one did it better!

With one swish of her ruby wand,
the post was marked to go

by **Bee Express**

(for super fast)

Whoooooosh

Juno Jewel
1ˢᵗ Treasure Street
Sparkle Town

Buzzzzz

Flutter
Flutter

or **Butterfly**

(safe, but slow).

Daphne Diamond
The Diamond Boutique
Sparkle Town

Flutter
Flutter

Rosie liked to work at speed; her post was **never** late.

But sometimes her deliveries reached the **wrong door,** house or **gate.**

At **Christmas**, Rosie whizzed and dashed.
She had no time to pause.

Her **toughest** task was sorting out
the letters for **Santa Claus!**

This year the post was stacked **sky-high** and, in a ruby flurry, she sent them off by **turtle dove**, marked:

Cupcake Parlour – PLEASE HURRY!

Cupcake Parlour? That's odd! Christmas letters usually go to the North Pole.

Turtle Dove Christmas Delivery No time to stop!

The next day, Rosie got a call:

"**Cupcake Parlour** here. You sent the Christmas post to us!"

Poor Rosie cried,

"OH, DEAR!"

"Whatever can I do?" she wailed.
"I used the **wrong address!**
And now the turtle doves are gone —
how will I fix this mess?"

Next, she searched the fairy web for someone else to help . . .

Hmm.

I can do it!

but then she suddenly realised: "I'm fast, I'll go MYSELF!"

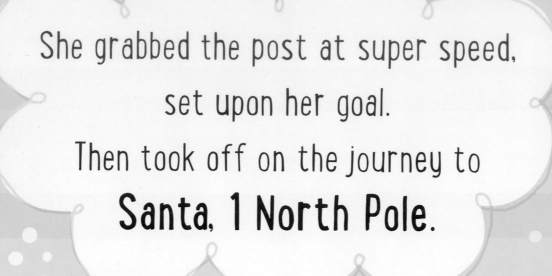

She grabbed the post at super speed,
set upon her goal.
Then took off on the journey to
Santa, 1 North Pole.

POST OFFICE

Good luck, Rosie!

Rosie **flew** in wind and snow,
with all her **flying force**.

Santa Claus
1 North Pole

But when she checked the map, she gasped,
"Oh, no! I've flown
OFF COURSE!"

"I **rushed** and got it wrong again," she cried out, feeling beat.
"I've **ruined** Christmas," Rosie sobbed.
But **then** came the pattering feet . . .

Santa Claus
1 North Pole

. . . of a **reindeer,** who smiled kindly

and said, "What can I do?"

She asked,

"Can you take me to Santa?"

Santa Claus
1 North Pole

He **nodded,** and off they flew.

Santa's house came into view,
and Rosie felt relieved.

Santa Claus
1 North Pole

She'd got there in the nick of time,
for today was **Christmas Eve!**

She knocked, and **Santa Claus** appeared!
He said, "Dear, please come in."

"I hope I'm not too late,"
she said.

CUPCAKE
SPRINKLES

Santa Claus
1 North Pole

"Of course not; **let's begin!**"

As Santa read each letter out, the elves made gifts with care.

And Rosie soon fell fast asleep
in Santa's snug, soft chair.

The night's stars **twinkled** in the sky.

The sleigh was ready at last.

Santa said, "We'll take my reindeer —

I promise that they're **fast!**"

When the sleigh reached Sparkle Town, the fairies gave a **cheer**.
"Before I go," said Santa, "I have one last **idea**."

Hooray!

"Close your eyes
and hold my hand,
then wave
your wand,"
he said...

And, just like that, the sky was filled
with **FIREWORKS** of ruby red!

In the twinkling of a fairy's wand, Santa flew away.

And Rosie snuggled into bed,
ready for **Christmas Day.**

Rosie learnt that when you rush,
you can sometimes get in trouble.

But if you **try** and **don't give in**,
you can work through **any** muddle!